# Bright Christmas

# Bright Christmas
## An Angel Remembers

by Andrew Clements ✳ Illustrated by Kate Kiesler

CLARION BOOKS ✳ New York

Clarion Books
a Houghton Mifflin Company imprint
215 Park Avenue South, New York, NY 10003
Text copyright © 1996 by Andrew Clements
Illustrations copyright © 1996 by Kate Kiesler

Title calligraphy by Iskra

The illustrations for this book were executed in oil paint.
The text is set in 16/20-point Hiroshige.

For information about this and other Houghton Mifflin trade and reference
books and multimedia products, visit The Bookstore at Houghton Mifflin
on the World Wide Web at (http://www.hmco.com/trade/).

Printed in the USA

**Library of Congress Cataloging-in-Publication Data**

Clements, Andrew, 1949–
Bright Christmas : an angel remembers / by Andrew Clements ; illustrated by Kate Kiesler.
p.    cm.
Summary: An angel who was present at the birth of Jesus remembers that very special night,
graced by heavenly light and an angelic song like the smile of God.
ISBN 0-395-72096-6
1. Jesus Christ—Nativity—Juvenile fiction.    [1. Jesus Christ—Nativity—Fiction.    2. Angels—Fiction.
3. Christmas—Fiction.]    I. Kiesler, Kate A., ill.    II. Title.
PZ7.C59118Br    1996
[E]—dc20    95-20371
CIP
AC

BVG    10  9  8  7  6  5  4  3  2

*For Anetta Schneider and Virginia Pettit*
—A.C.

*To Anne Diebel,*
*for her encouragement and enthusiasm*
—K.K.

I have always been an angel. Always.
I've never needed a clock or a calendar,
because here where I live
there's really no time at all.
So I guess it's strange for me
to remember a certain night.
But I do remember.
Because that night was different
from all the others—ever.
That night, the great truth
came to the earth once and for all.

People sometimes think that Christmas
came suddenly, one holy night.
I know better.
Other things came first—
amazing things, beautiful things,
important things.
And I saw them all.
Because when a message goes from heaven to earth,
it's not a letter.
It's an angel.
And the angel doesn't just *carry* the message.
The angel *is* the message.

We had brought light and truth
to the earth before that night.
Why?
Earth needed to be ready.
We sang to Moses,
and then Moses was given commandments
that brought the great truth closer.
We sang to David,
and when David saw that the great truth
would come to earth through his own family,
he sang too—psalm after psalm after psalm.
We sang to Isaiah,
and Isaiah saw that the great truth
would come as a child—
he would be called Prince of Peace,
Wonderful, Counselor.

But still, earth seemed dark and far away.
Until that night.
That night, a light was lit like no other.

I remember the star in the sky above Bethlehem.
All the songs and messages
we had ever brought to earth—
they all led up to that one night,
and they lit up the sky.

We were watching over Joseph and his wife
when the innkeeper sent them away.
We knew where they were going.
We knew they would be safe and warm
in the quiet of the stable.

In the hills above Bethlehem,
I remember the faces of the shepherds, looking up.
It was time for the great truth to shine on the earth.
Nothing could have stopped it,
and nothing could have kept us
from singing about it.
And sing we did—
"Glory to God in the highest,
and on earth peace,
good will toward men.
For unto you is born this day
in the city of David a Savior,
which is Christ the Lord."

And nothing could have kept those shepherds
from walking through the night to see the child.
We lit the path,
and like sheep that had been lost
the shepherds found their way.

And Mary.
I will always remember her face
when she heard us sing.
Mary knew that this child,
laid in a manger,
was bringing the great truth.
She knew it in her heart,
and it shone in her face that night.

Earth now had a heavenly light of its own,
and it made me sing louder and sweeter.
Our song was like the smile of God.
And the light and the music and the angels
were the same thing,
and Jesus smiled too.
The light shined in the darkness,
and there was no night there.
I remember.

Here where we live, there's really no time at all.
It's just now—the day in heaven.
And right now in the day in heaven,
it is still that first Christmas night.

Once I sing a song, the song never stops.
It's like a star that burns forever.
Christmas is the brightest
and the happiest song I ever sang.
The star is still shining,
and I am still singing,
and the earth is still singing back.

## A Note

Angels appear frequently in the Bible. Whenever God decided to play a part in the affairs of the people on earth, an angel was sent to tell the news. The most detailed account of the story of the birth of Jesus is found in the first two chapters of The Gospel According to Luke. In it, the angel Gabriel appears to Mary to announce the coming birth of the holy child, who would be called the Son of God. In telling the story of the Nativity from the angels' point of view, Andrew Clements faithfully presents the Good News in the spirit of the biblical account.

Great care has been taken by artist Kate Kiesler to place the story in the Holy Land as archeological study tells us it looked at the time of Jesus' birth. Bethlehem was a small hillside village of flat-roofed stone houses, with shepherds' fields nearby. The village was too small to have had proper inns where large numbers of travelers could stay. The inn shown here is a *kataluma*, or "temporary shelter," a large marquee used by the Romans to house people when permanent accommodations were not available. It is thought that the stable where Jesus was born was a cave used by shepherds to house their sheep. The Church of the Nativity, one of the oldest churches in the world, is built over the cave and can still be seen by visitors to Bethlehem.